This book
belongs to:

....

....

EGMONT

We bring stories to life

First published in Great Britain 2007
by Egmont UK Limited
239 Kensington High Street, London W8 6SA
BARBIE and associated trademarks and trade dress are owned by,
and used under license from, Mattel, Inc.
© 2007, Mattel, Inc.

ISBN 978 1 4052 2998 2
ISBN 1 4052 2998 5

1 3 5 7 9 10 8 6 4 2

Printed in Italy

Based on the original screenplay by Elise Allen.

Special thanks to Rob Hudnut, Tiffany J. Shuttleworth, Vicki Jaeger, Monica Okazaki, Luke Carroll, Cherish Bryck, Anita Lee, Kelly Shin, Pam Prostarr, Dave Lee, James Wallace, Tricia Jellis, Aeron Kline, Zoe Evamy, Steve Lumley, Shaun Martens, Lil Reichmann, Derek Toye, Sheila Turner, Eric Cheung, Peter Donnelly, Behzad Mansoori-Dara, Joel Olmstead, Craig Shiells, and Walter Martishius

*E*lina is the most famous fairy in all of Fairytopia!

Not long ago, the seven Guardians who watch over Fairytopia were kidnapped by the evil Laverna. But thanks to Elina's bravery, the Guardians were freed, and Laverna's evil plan to become queen of Fairytopia was foiled. Now Laverna is imprisoned in the Bogs of the Hinterland, and Elina is a heroine. All the young pixies look up to her, and pester her for stories.

One day, Elina is playing with her puffball friend, Bibble, when the pixies come up to them.

"You're my heroine!" cries one little pixie. Her eyes sparkle as she gazes at Elina.

"Will you tell us about the times you saved Fairytopia?" begs another.

Elina blushes. All this admiration is nice, but it makes her a little bit nervous.

But the pixies won't get to hear the story today. Elina hears a familiar voice behind her – and there is Azura, one of the seven Guardians.

Azura wants to talk in private, so they go to a quiet glade.

"Each Guardian has been asked by the Enchantress to pick an apprentice," Azura says. She looks Elina straight in the eyes. "I'd like to choose you."

"Wow…" Elina falters, taken aback. "I mean… that is… I'm honoured!"

Azura smiles. "I'm glad. You'll live in the Crystal Palace, and learn the Flight of Spring. It's a very important dance, which releases the First Blush of Spring."

What they don't realise is that Laverna has been listening! One of her evil helpers, a Fungus, is lurking behind a leaf. He has a magic medallion that lets Laverna hear everything.

"Follow Elina!" the evil fairy commands him. "And try to blend in! I don't want anyone to know you're there!"

"Yes, your Wartiness," replies the Fungus obediently. He's almost as scared of his evil mistress as the fairies are.

Elina and Bibble are on their way to the Crystal Palace when they hear a strange voice.

"It's OK, little guy," says the voice. "Come on…"

They look around, but they can't see anyone until Bibble flies around a corner. There, in a glade, is a male fairy with handsome green wings. He's talking to an adorable baby Pooka.

"Awwww!" squeaks Bibble.

Oops! The Pooka hears Bibble, and rears up in fright. Linden quickly glances round to see where the noise came from.

Poor Elina is embarrassed, but fortunately Linden doesn't mind the interruption. In fact, it turns out he's an apprentice too, so he's glad to meet her.

The Pooka calms down and whinnies at Elina. Linden smiles and pats the little creature on the head.

"I'm an Oread, so I can speak animal language," Linden explains.

"He says his name is Tumby, and he likes you!"

Elina likes Tumby too, but she's worried about arriving late at the Crystal Palace.

"I have to get to the dorms," she apologises to Linden. "I have to meet everyone some time, I suppose."

"I can go with you," Linden offers, but Elina shakes her head.

"I want to do it by myself," she says. "I have to be strong."

The dorms turn out to be amazing. Each one is a living flower that glows with magical light.

"Hi," says Elina, peering nervously through the petals of the first flower. "I'm Elina, and this is Bibble."

Inside the room is an elegant blue fairy and a small pink pixie. The pixie stares rudely at Elina.

"We're not interested in having uninvited guests," she snaps.

Elina smiles uncomfortably and flies out. The next room she tries is bright orange, and sitting on the bed is Sunburst the Sparkle Fairy.

"Oh, you must be Elina," she says.

"Yes, I am!" cries Elina, relieved to find someone friendly.

"Bummer," says Sunburst, wrinkling up her nose. "I was hoping you wouldn't show. Listen, Miss I-Saved-Fairytopia, I don't buy the idea that we should all bow down to you."

"What?" cries Elina. "But I don't buy it either!"

"Listen to that," Sunburst sneers. "Here I am, just sitting in my room, and you barge in yelling. I think you should go now."

Sadly, Elina starts to leave the dorms. But on her way out, Glee, the Nature Fairy, invites Elina to her room. What a relief for Elina to meet someone friendly!

Lessons start the next day. The first class is Magic, and Sunburst immediately starts showing off how clever she is. She stretches out her hand, and fire sparks from her necklace.

When Elina's turn comes, she makes a waterfall flow from her necklace. Everyone is impressed, except Sunburst.

"When Sparkle Fairies touch water, we lose all our powers!" she cries. "Cut it out!"

"I don't know how," Elina stammers.

"I don't believe you!" Sunburst snarls.

The teacher has to make the waterfall vanish. Now Sunburst thinks Elina deliberately attacked her.

The next lesson is Flance, a special combination of flight and dance that the fairies perform during the Flight of Spring.

Bibble, and Glee's puffball friend Dizzle, come to class to support their friends. But Elina is very nervous when she has to Flance in front of everyone. The teacher stares at her in silence, and she feels miserable.

"Was it that horrible?" she asks.

"Elina," replies her teacher. "That was incredible!"

"Show off!" hisses Faben, a male fairy with purple wings. Elina tries not to take any notice of the nasty comment. Faben might be handsome, but he dances like a Fungus!

That evening, Elina goes for a walk with Linden. He's a good friend, and listens to her sympathetically.

"Sunburst hated me from the minute we met," she sighs. "It seems like everything I do only makes it worse. I don't think the others like me either."

"Are you kidding?" Linden protests. "You're probably the most talented apprentice here. But if you're worried, talk to Azura about it."

"No," Elina shakes her head. "That would make me seem weak."

Suddenly, a toad hops onto Linden's foot.

"The poor thing!" Elina exclaims. "It's limping."

"She says she's from the Bogs of the Hinterlands," Linden translates the toad's croaks. "She's been exiled by a wicked fairy."

"Laverna!" gasps Elina.

The toad tells Linden that the curse can only be broken by fairy undoing magic.

Immediately, Elina does the spell, and the toad changes shape. But she doesn't turn into an ordinary fairy – Elina has been tricked into releasing Laverna!

"Hello again, my dear," she sneers. "You've just signed the death warrant for Fairytopia as you know it!"

As Elina and Linden stare in horror, Laverna takes off into the sky.

Elina and Linden rush back to tell the Guardians, who are very worried. They increase security at the Crystal Palace.

In the apprentices' common room, the other fairies are angry with Elina for releasing Laverna – all except Sunburst, who gives Elina a hug.

"I'm sorry," says Sunburst. "I'm sure you didn't mean for this to happen."

Then the Sparkle Fairy flies off to her room, leaving Elina and Linden very surprised.

"I guess disaster brings out the best in her!" exclaims Linden.

Things get even worse when Elina receives a mysterious note telling her to meet Laverna alone in the forest for a showdown. When she goes to the woods, nobody is there. But when she comes back to the Palace she finds Azura unconscious.

Elina is horrified. She was supposed to be on patrol, and the note was a fake to draw her away. While she was gone, Laverna fought off Sunburst and poisoned all the Guardians!

"But it's not Elina's fault," says Sunburst. "Laverna's just so powerful! Probably the most powerful fairy – ever!"

Elina wonders why Sunburst is being so nice. And why does she sound like she admires Laverna?

With all the Guardians unconscious, the apprentices must perform the Flight of Spring. For two days they practise their hardest, and finally the moment arrives.

Everyone gathers in the courtyard of the Crystal Palace. The Enchantress, seated on her throne, raises her hand, and the apprentices cast their first spell. Beautiful, coloured walls of water shoot up from the waterways in the courtyard, forming the Rainbow Dome. The magic has begun!

The apprentices chant their first spell. Inside the safety of the dome, a fragile flower begins to bloom – the First Blush of Spring.

Elina is nervous, but determined. If the apprentices don't perform the Flight of Spring, Fairytopia will be doomed.

"Isn't it exciting?" says Sunburst to Elina.

"Very," Elina agrees. "I wonder if we can do it?"

"Of course we can," Sunburst grins. "You wouldn't let some limping toad get in your way, right?"

Elina frowns. "How did you know the toad limped?" she asks slowly. "I never told anyone that…"

She looks hard into Sunburst's eyes and suddenly realises the truth. This is no Sparkle Fairy – it's Laverna!

Elina flies out of the Rainbow Dome, ignoring the shouts of the other fairies. They must continue the Flance without her. She has to find the real Sunburst.

But how? Fairytopia is a huge place. Elina hovers over the fields, bewildered.

"I must think where Sunburst could be!" she scolds herself. Then she has an idea. "Water!" she cries. "Sunburst's a Sparkle Fairy, so Laverna would have put her in water!"

Elina hurries towards the river that runs through the meadows of Fairytopia.

Far under the water, something orange catches her eye. Sunburst's wing! Elina summons her courage, and dives. She swims down to the riverbed, then drags the Sparkle Fairy to the surface.

Sunburst sits on the bank, recovering from Laverna's trance spell.

"Elina?" she mutters. Then she comes round and her eyes widen. "Laverna! She –"

"I know," Elina interrupts. "And it's worse than you think. We have to get back to the Palace!"

Elina and Sunburst fly into the Rainbow Dome.

"That's not Sunburst!" cries Elina, pointing to Laverna.

The evil fairy's eyes swirl as her body changes back into its own form. She moves her hands, creating a pulsing bubble of light.

"Step inside this spell chamber," Laverna orders the Enchantress.

"In there, all your powers will be useless. Fairytopia will be mine!"

The apprentices cry out in dismay, but the Enchantress has no choice. As soon as her sister is inside the bubble, Laverna fires poisonous magic at the First Blush of Spring.

Elina throws herself in front of the flower just in time.

"Together we're strong!" she shouts to the other apprentices.

"I'll pick you off one at a time," Laverna sneers.

But Sunburst understands what Elina means. "We won't be coming for you one at a time!"

One by one, each fairy throws her light into Elina. Shining beams of colour flow from Elina's hands and push Laverna's evil power back towards her.

"No!" shrieks Laverna. But the rainbow energy is stronger than her darkness. There's an explosion, and the evil fairy disappears.

Elina falls to the ground, exhausted. Her friends gather round anxiously.

"Are you OK?" asks Sunburst.

Elina struggles to her feet – and everyone gasps in astonishment. Elina's wings have grown bigger, and they sparkle with all the colours of the rainbow!

"It's because you acted so bravely," explains the Enchantress. "You asked for help when you needed it. Your fellow apprentices were there for you, and now they're part of you forever."

But Elina has seen something that makes her forget her wings.

"The First Blush of Spring!" she cries. "It's wilted!"

"That's it," groans Faben. "Fairytopia's doomed."

"No, we still have a chance," the Enchantress corrects him. "Gather together, apprentices."

The fairies form a circle around the wilted flower. Their energy builds, then wraps itself around the Blush, healing it to its former glory. Fairytopia is saved, all thanks to Elina – and her friends.

A few weeks later, it's the end of term. The apprentices gather at the Crystal Palace to receive their magic necklaces from the Enchantress.

"I am honoured to know you all," she says. "I thank you, and Fairytopia thanks you."

When it's time for everyone to say goodbye, Sunburst is a bit sheepish. She's obviously hoping Elina will forgive her nasty behaviour.

"I do have one question," she says. "How did you know it was Laverna doing the Flight of Spring?"

"Easy," Elina replies. "Laverna was nice to me!"

The two fairies grin at each other and share a hug before Sunburst flies away.

"I made you something," Elina says to Linden a bit nervously. She takes out a sparkling necklace. "It's a prism. It makes rainbows, so you'll always remember me."

"Thanks," replies Linden, smiling shyly. "I made you something too. A Tumby bracelet. So you don't forget me either."

"I never could," Elina promises.

As Elina spreads her beautiful wings, a rainbow rises in the sky, and all the apprentices hover in front of it to wave goodbye. Elina is sorry to leave but she remembers the Enchantress's words – her friends will be part of her forever.

WIN with Barbie™

Barbie Fairytopia™

Star Prize!

Barbie™ Fairytopia Bicycle and Accessories!

You've got places to go! Now get there in style with this beautiful Barbie bicycle! This bike is the finest in cycle chic and with your matching Barbie accessories your safety is ensured as well!

5 to win!

Magic of the Rainbow Barbie™ doll AND jewellery box!

The first 5 runners-up will receive not only a fabulous NEW Magic of the Rainbow Barbie™ doll but also a jewellery box, where you can keep all your amazing fashion accessories.

5 to win!

Magic of the Rainbow Barbie™ doll!

The next 5 runners-up will receive a fabulous NEW Magic of the Rainbow Barbie™ doll!

To enter the competition, just draw and colour in a picture of Barbie, fill in your details on this form and send the entry panel, remembering to keep the terms and conditions, together with your drawing to: Barbie™ Magic of the Rainbow Competition, Egmont UK Ltd, 239 Kensington High Street, London, W8 6SA.
This Barbie™ Magic of the Rainbow competition closes on 30th September 2007.

Name:_____

Child's Age:_____   Email:_____

Address:_____

_____

_____ Postcode:_____

Parent's / Guardian's Signature:_____

Please tick here ☐ if you are happy for Egmont UK Ltd to contact you in future to inform you of goods or services related to their brands that may be of interest to you.

EGMONT

We bring stories to life